Alfred Tennyson

Song of the Brook

With Illus. by A.F. Bellows

Alfred Tennyson

Song of the Brook
With Illus. by A.F. Bellows

ISBN/EAN: 9783744767347

Printed in Europe, USA, Canada, Australia, Japan

Cover: Foto ©Andreas Hilbeck / pixelio.de

More available books at **www.hansebooks.com**

SONG OF THE BROOK.

PUBLISHERS' NOTICE.

*This volume is the initial one of a series, which will be
entitled* "SONGS FROM THE GREAT POETS."

BY

ALFRED TENNYSON, D.C.L.

*WITH ILLUSTRATIONS BY A. F. BELLOWS, J. D. WOODWARD,
MISS L. B. HUMPHREY, AND F. B. SCHELL.*

BOSTON:

PUBLISHED BY ESTES AND LAURIAT.

1888.

SONG OF THE BROOK.

LIST OF ILLUSTRATIONS.

SONG OF THE BROOK.

I.

I come from haunts of coot and hern,
  I make a sudden sally
And sparkle out among the fern,
  To bicker down a valley.

By thirty hills I hurry down,
  Or slip between the ridges,
By twenty thorps, a little town,
  And half a hundred bridges.

Till last by Philip's farm I flow
  To join the brimming river;
For men may come and men may go,
  But I go on forever.

II.

I chatter over stony ways,
  In little sharps and trebles;
I bubble into eddying bays,
  I babble on the pebbles.

With many a curve my banks I fret
  By many a field and fallow,
And many a fairy foreland set
  With willow-weed and mallow.

I chatter, chatter, as I flow,
  To join the brimming river;
For men may come and men may go,
  But I go on forever.

III.

I wind about, and in and out,
  With here a blossom sailing,
And here and there a lusty trout,
  And here and there a grayling,

And here and there a foamy flake
  Upon me, as I travel
With many a silvery waterbreak
  Above the golden gravel,

And draw them all along, and flow
  To join the brimming river;
For men may come and men may go,
  But I go on forever.

IV.

I steal by lawns and grassy plots,
  I slide by hazel covers;
I move the sweet forget-me-nots
  That grow for happy lovers.

I slip, I slide, I gloom, I glance,
  Among my skimming swallows;
I make the netted sunbeam dance
  Against my sandy shallows.

I murmur under moon and stars
  In brambly wildernesses;
I linger by my shingly bars,
  I loiter round my cresses;

And out again I curve and flow
  To join the brimming river;
For men may come and men may go,
  But I go on forever.

I come from haunts of coot and hern,
    I make a sudden sally
And sparkle out among the fern,
    To bicker down a valley.

By thirty hills I hurry down,
    Or slip between the ridges,
By twenty thorps, a little town,
    And half a hundred bridges.

Till last by Philip's farm I flow

To
  join the
    brimming
      river;
   For men may come and men may go,
    But I go on forever.

I chatter over stony ways,
    In little sharps and trebles;
I bubble into eddying bays,
    I babble on the pebbles.

With many a curve my banks I fret
　　By many a field and fallow,
And many a fairy foreland set
　　With willow-weed and mallow.

I chatter, chatter, as I flow,
    To join the brimming river;
For men may come and men may go,
    But I go on forever.

I wind about, and in and out,
With here a blossom sailing,

And here and there a lusty trout,
And here and there a grayling,

And here
and there
a foamy flake
Upon me, as I travel
With many a silvery waterbreak
Above the golden gravel,

And draw them all along, and flow
        To join the brimming river;
For men may come and men may go,
        But I go on forever.

I steal by lawns and grassy plots,

I slide by hazel covers;

I move the sweet forget-me-nots
That grow for happy lovers.

I slip, I slide, I gloom, I glance,
    Among my skimming swallows;
I make the netted sunbeam dance
    Against my sandy shallows.

I murmur under moon and stars
    In brambly wildernesses;
I linger by my shingly bars,
    I loiter round my cresses;

And out again I curve and flow
　　To join the brimming river;
For men may come and men may go,
　　But I go on forever.